THE JOURNAL OF MISKA KORPI

PYRO ACE

The Journal of Miska Korpi
Copyright © 2024 by Pyro Ace.

MILTON & HUGO L.L.C.
4407 Park Ave., Suite 5
Union City, NJ 07087, USA

Website: *www. miltonandhugo.com*
Hotline: *1- 888-778-0033*
Email: *info@miltonandhugo.com*

Ordering Information:
Quantity sales. Special discounts are granted to corporations, associations, and other organizations. For more information on these discounts, please reach out to the publisher using the contact information provided above.

Library of Congress Control Number: 2024919760
ISBN-13:   979-8-89285-257-9   [Paperback Edition]
                 979-8-89285-258-6   [Digital Edition]

Rev. date: 08/27/2024

CONTENTS

I

The start of sailing

The air emulated salt and heat. The beautiful sun warmed it all around me as I peered through the window of passion. It captivated me and my hopes almost perfectly. What I dreamt of throughout the night, what I wanted from life, what I thought my life would be forever, and – the most important one – who I felt I was.

The glimmering clear sky allowing the sun to say hello gave me determination to make the most of the meaningful day. The scenery just seems too grand to be true. Water rings and crashes against the small ship docked just meters from my half-open window.

The rocking of the vessel calling for use under the beautiful bright and sunny day. I stand up in my perfect life; just as I dreamt as a kid. I have a little metal tin ready from the night before that I bring with me everywhere.

It's full of the wonders and things I grew up with. These things make my days better and longer. I adore them. 'I mustn't forget them,' I think as they drop into my black hole of a pocket. I eagerly get ready for a day of sailing. I wonder if my crew is too. Typically, I am left waiting for them.

On my short, very short, trip to the edge of the dock, I felt a bit hungry and thirsty. I recall a quick breakfast spot nearby, just shy the edge of town specifically. I detest the café like appeal, but I make my way there anyway.

Soon after ordering, I checked my watch and noticed I'm nearly keeping them waiting now. I shrug it off and pick up my morning snack and energy. Upon stepping outside, I see the two special crewmen standing at the dock awaiting my presence. I walk over and greet them under the beaming sun.

"What happened to being punctual? Are you now trying to allow life to pass you by?" The older, rougher friend Jarmo exclaims with a light chuckle.

"No, Jarmo, I'm not. I grew hungry waiting. Sorry to keep you standing." I returned the favor with a light laugh.

"I understand that. I've done it a few times on my walk here." The younger Olari says to us both. He's been bad with punctuality for as long as I knew him.

"Well, now that we're all 'ere. Let's get going, no?" Jarmo exclaims while stepping on the dock.

"Very well! Step in you two, I'll tend to the knot." Olari stepped in carefully with his bag and rod cautiously set down.

His clean, young hand guided Jarmo in too. Olari was always cautious and thought too much. Frankly, he reminded me of someone I used to be but learnt that people used niceness as a gateway to manipulation.

Jarmo's older joints crackling and wearing as he brings himself down into the vessel. Jarmo always traveled light as most of what was helpful in the moment was forgotten hours early when packing. Never could he ever remember something long term.

Must have been his age catching up with him the last few years. Olari, however, always was grand at over-preparing. His bag was packed with refreshments and snacks for each of us. I carefully tended to the knot that kept this vessel stable and stepped in with the help of both friends. We all wore the same outfit.

A traditional sailor fits with a tucked, breathable scarf around the collars of the shirts. However, mine being used the last few years had wear and tear, Jarmo's having some strings and stains on his had it been his forever at this point, and finally Olari's being super new. I think he bought it yesterday, honestly. With all that considered and the crew back together. I look out to the open waters and take a deep breath. Here we go, another day, another adventure. Here's to a longer adventure than ever before.

-Miska Korpi, 1999.

II

Where am I?

A loud beeping played rhythmically. My eyes opened to see the world beyond me not of salty air or brightening sun, but a room with dim lights and tubes in my arms. Where was my hopeful sun with the blue skies asking for me to be on a vessel under them? The lack of salty air felt wrong to be in. The purity was overwhelming and taking over my sailor nose.

"Where am I? What is this place?" My voice, rough, squeezed, and cleared up.

"Mister Korpi, you're up again. How pleasant. You're in the hospital. Same as weeks prior." A voice around the corner called upon my prompting questions with a sound of graphite being grinded to a paper.

"But I was..."

"...just with Jarmo Lahtinen and Olari Honka." The voice around the corner interrupted as if it was tired of awaiting me to say the entire sentence.

"How did you know?"

"It's the same as every other. I've done so much digging and still only get those names from you. Those people don't exist."

"But I just untied the knot holding my vessel to my dock. I don't understand." I thought of my words much more carefully in this unfamiliar place. I didn't want to say anything wrong or offensive in a place not kindly taking me in. I attempted to sit up but failed. "How is it possible?" I continued to chase into the confusion and uncertainty of where I truly was held. My head started hurting in this bed of prison bars that held me from standing up from the sides.

"I cannot disclose to you just yet. We've not found out why, Miska."

"Why not?"

"The doctor is still uncertain about what he thinks. We don't wish to give you false information, so when he is most certain, we will speak." The voice said with a hint of annoyance. The voice's exhaustion peered through. The silence in the room grew with my thoughts disappearing. My chest had found a sudden hurt the longer I sat quietly.

"You should just go back to sleep; nobody is coming to visit today. They are all out working."

"Who? - Actually, never mind." I responded with. "What about my wife?"

"You are married?" the voice asked with genuine confusion. Almost as if the idea of me having a wife has never been brought forward on paper or verbally.

"Do I?" Now that I thought about it, I can't remember myself.

"I never had any record of it, I'll do some research on your relationships while you rest. I'll see you tomorrow or tonight, whichever comes first."

"What about my metal tin that I had?"

"I don't know why you believe that you would be allowed to have those in here, but in case you forgot – which you did – they were taken months ago upon your first arrival, Miska."

I gave up and plopped my head on my pillow, staring at the ceiling in defeat. What's going on with me? Just like that, I rest my eyes with a deep sigh, nothing is coming back to me. Where was I with Jarmo? Who are Jarmo and Olari?

-Miska Korpi, 2000

He awoke, but I just grabbed at the pencil sitting on my desk around the corner from him. He started speaking to me. I charted down the vitals and his responses and actions once he woke. However, I discreetly wrote down this entry for my personal documentation.

Upon his awakening, however, I got the same old crap I always got from him. This has been going on for way longer than it should have. I have never had a patient wait this long for a diagnosis. The doctor must be hiding something from me because he is scared or worried, I wouldn't want to provide service for Miska anymore.

For the last few months, he's been here and under my care, I cannot say he had more than one week total of not saying or asking these questions. What do you even tell someone at that point? When someone just wakes up every single day asking, "where am I" and "where is my metal tin"?

How dare you think you would be able to have that in here? This is a medically professional environment, and he chooses to want his drugs? What do you tell them after a while? Am I supposed to lie? I am chasing tails in circles and squares, triangles and spheres.

I cannot find any facts or even records of the people he keeps asking for. The doctor hasn't even given me a word to say about his condition to him. I find him an anomaly because he is missing a large chunk of his hip and still perfectly fine. How has he not died from blood loss?

I guess that until he does have some sort of issue from those symptoms that he is my responsibility the entire time. Although, I should probably not let him have the pencil in case he does hurt himself or me with it. I don't think he would remember he had a pencil, but I still cannot risk any chances that he would do something. It is also for my safety that he doesn't stab me with it.

-Nurse Härkören, 2000

III

The Journey

After sailing for an hour - give or take - we reached our fishing spot; it was just a few miles off the coast. Jarmo was eager to cast, but I couldn't blame him. It gets irritable when you just sit in a small vessel for a bit. I kind of had a headache from the heat over the water and the salty scent radiating above, among other things, but they wouldn't want to be a part of it either.

"You goin' to cast it in?" Jarmo broke the silence by asking me with a quick side-eye.

"Unsure… a thought hitting me now is… what if something large hits the small vessel of mine we are fishing from?" I spoke concerned.

"And that right there is why I have more fun." He replied with his eyes glued to his little bobber.

"What are you on about? I do have fun, no?" My voice chimed up with a perplexing rasp.

"You both - youngens - think too much. Olari and Miska, the young souls cursed with thinking too much rather than just having fun." He rambled on and on and I gave up listening.

"I may be older, but I just live life free of over-thinking and fear. You only see this beautiful planet one time." He spat while actually looking between the both of us rather than his rod.

"I'm just fishing, old man. I like and enjoy what I actually do." Olari piped up with a chuckle. I joined in on the laugh and responded carefully. The words made me think about how I will go on in life. What I truly like and do. Do I really think too much? That is why I keep the metal tin with me every day. It helps me think less and act more radically to enjoy myself while still be conservative and respectful. It brings my mind to slow down and process things properly.

"I guess you're right. Let's fish. However, if I was right, I'm hitting you in the afterlife, Jarmo."

"You won't find me there, but sure." He responded, keeping his smile up.

"Why not?"

"Just not my fancy but forget about it and have fun. You're thinking too much again."

"Anyone hungry?" Olari broke the conversation with food.

"Sure, why not?" Jarmo spoke, also deterring from the prior conversation.

"I got one for each of us. E'erybody's favorite." Olari smiled while rummaging in his bag.

"Näkkileipä?" I inquired eagerly. Food would help my mind calm down too, I loved when he offered me something.

"Of course! What else do you like on a fishing trip?" His response was followed by a small bag with crisp bread in it.

One for each of us. Nothing was biting anyway, so each of our attention spans went elsewhere. While the sun had set, we decided to do something that diverted our plan. Between snacking, cracking some jokes, babbling about life, and not catching anything Jarmo's solo bag contained a mini pop-up tent for a camping night too.

"Good thing you are off tomorrow, Miska." He said after revealing his own plan. His voice trailed off after a word I barely heard, 'indefinitely.'

"I suppose it works, but what did you say after?" I inquired eagerly with genuine concern.

"Don't you go on hearing things now, ya crazy." Jarmo said while waving off my question.

"I know you said something else. I'm not crazy." A biting tone of annoyance erupted slowly in my voice.

"He said nothing more. Calm down, bud. We are all friends chilling on a fishing trip." Olari tries to dilute the annoyance in my voice. Shortly after, I apologize. We want to wake up earlier tomorrow, so we rest under the beautiful stars.

-Miska Korpi, 1999

He keeps writing in this book, but I cannot find it when he asleep. I checked under the bed, in the bed, when I take his sheets to wash, the little table next to the bed, even the machinery that monitors him while he rests, and I cannot find it anywhere. No other patient has hidden anything from me this well. It might answer some questions about what he is thinking, how, when, of who even! I just want to find out what happened, what is wrong, what can I do?

I am failing this patient because of the anomaly that is him. Even when I had another patient at their home that was aged, and deteriorating were they easier than this not even middle-aged man. I might need to bring him something abnormal from the exterior world.

I have records of his parents, although I found a death document for his father. As per the record, the case was really messy and heavily investigated, but it was found that he took his own life and left a note that the inheritance goes to his son.

Miska was an only child, and that was what I was looking for. Oh, wait, no, I was looking for a document pertaining to marriage. He didn't handle the death well from the background and officer reporting upon his first arrival.

That metal tin he always cries about was confiscated and documented. Upon his discharge, he is meant to meet with an officer outside of our care. Miska Korpi inherited money from his father that he seemed to have magically lost and refused to pay tax on because he claimed to never have received it. I'll keep looking and continue documenting the findings down by hand as these informal writings shouldn't enter the computer. This is a vent document and sign off.

-Nurse Härkören, 2000

IV

Am I crazy?

When I woke, the sky was cloudy. The beautiful sun was saying 'hi there' again. The sun is always a reliable thing. The set of clouds was moving and brushing the sky like a cleanup crew. My bones weren't aching as I sat up and headed outside of the tent.

My head hurt though as I didn't sleep very well on that camping trip. It was still before the fullest sunrise. I sat back against a tall, full tree with my back. The water seemed to be as peaceful as a childhood memory.

I grasped my metal tin and opened it. I took one of the rolls out that I prepared and enjoyed it. A peaceful, little fish swam up with its scales glowing a bright glimmer of royalty. The slim nature of the fish as if it was the "species standard" helped it seem so effortless to approach a human. The beady eyes of this fish ensuring its safety to deliver me itself. The fish said to me out of nowhere.

"You - man of the dream land with skies so grand. Why do you shun the life you hold in hand? In boundless blue, you should pursue. Yet – I fail to understand why you allow shadows to linger, obscuring thy view. While I - in currents of course - find my peace.

In the tranquil depths of black and blue, my worries cease." It spoke slowly and eerily. It was careful but confident in the words it delivered to me. Nothing was left askew but still was not quite level.

I leaned in closer to that mysterious fish that spoke to me. Oh, how that sounded so sincerely insane! "Does the sea's rush bring you cheer? Does the sunlight's dance enlighten you more?" It said to me. I rub my eyes and question my sanity even more than before.

"I think so?" I responded to this philosopher of fish in nature. How I still wonder why this fish was delivering this message to me. Was I truly something wrong in the world? A stain on humanity as it knew? Was I so messed up even fish could tell from the sea?

"Then why scorn life's grace? When there are creatures and people less fortunate?"

"I don't hate my life. I am having fun with my friends and sailing..." I had responded with genuine confusion and an edge of doubt. The blank eyes of the fish didn't grant me any peace about this interaction with nature. The fish said nothing, as it abruptly turned away and swam. Soon after the crazy hallucination, Olari and Jarmo walked out of the tent and approached the big peaceful tree I sat under. I had finished and disposed of my habit and tin before they approached. I ensured that I respected them in that of not flaunting my belongings.

"Ready for the day of the sea, brother?" Olari asked me upon seeing my genuine fear and concern. He always did worry for my wellbeing more than I did. He made sure that I was comfortable while still giving me a hard time. Never a day less do I wish I spent with him.

"I guess I am. I am as ready as I will ever be." I answered him as I stood up to start the day. I thought about what was said to me that day. I still do. For that was never articulated to me ever again. The words of wisdom from nature herself giving me advice. Why couldn't I receive that advice earlier thought? I wish I could hear and ask more. I – in this minute – ask myself why had I not listened to the fish more in depth. Maybe even asked these questions prior and made more educated decisions in my life? I'm running out of today's journal entry. Goodbye, journal.

- Miska Korpi, 1999

⤳

He has some interesting fantasies. I do not know what truly goes on in his mind. I wish there was a more involved way I could hear what a patient is thinking, so that I would be able to deliver the best care possible for them. Think of how easy it would be to see inside someone's mind when you are trying to deliver the best words of advice, response, action, or even a want they have.

Like, wouldn't it be easier to just see it than try to decipher the enigma they ever so carefully chose to say? Though, I guess that would take all the fun out of my job, huh. If we had technology like that, I would not ever have to talk to a patient.

Monitoring would be easy as I just look at the machine, no, projector of their memories and thoughts on the wall. Though, I would be sadder watching the patients in their last conversations before surgeries they don't believe they might make it through. If I had to watch the memories of my mom before she went, I think I would not have the motivation to go on.

Is that why I am so connected but resentful of this man? Do I think he is like my mom and wish he would just stop? I don't think I do, but nobody is ever right about the world. I miss my mom, and I wish I could see what she truly thought of me before she had gone. I watched a grown woman who had kids deteriorate in her own home. A safe place that she kept full of dreamcatchers and crosses to feel safe and happy.

The home she made with remedies to always bring something forward worth bringing forward. The air in that house during her last years just grew stronger and stronger. Those crosses she once had to bring the good times to you flipped one at a time.

The air grabbed ahold of your throat and wept in your face. It held on and made sure you knew that it was your time to feel sad too. Nobody truly understands what it means to say that you watched someone deteriorate in front of your very eyes.

For a mask to be forcibly put onto a person and they must act with it. A prison cell holding someone going through a persona change. It changes someone permanently until they breathe their final breath. I don't think I'd be who I was if she lived the life that she was supposed to. I wrote too much again. I might scrap this note. It is laughing at me and is vulnerable.

-Nurse Härkören, 2000

V

A Day I remember

"He's gotten worse, Doctor." she said to the doctor urgently. "He hasn't been cooperating in his medicines. He says they will make him worse. The bite on his hip is dying, but he lives without it. That makes no sense to me! How can he live with that on him? Should we perform surgery? Should we start some other, stronger treatment?"

"Who did, Nurse Härkören?" He inquired. "How can I make a decision without knowing the patient you are telling me to work on?"

"Miska Korpi did. You need to figure his case out, Doctor, I cannot keep telling him nothing is wrong." she scolded and sternly stated. "He sees it himself! He wakes up multiple times in the day with the same spiel every time! He asks for those two people I told you names and described in his words how they look, but they do not exist!"

He sighed and picked up a wide folder from the counter of the office.

"You see this folder, bossy?" He sarcastically said.

"That's not polite nor professional. Address me with my title as I earned it the same way." she said as she reached for the folder. "I have been watching this man suffer with no answers from you. That's almost hitting medical malpractice if it hasn't already!"

"Take it and read it." He said as he rolled his eyes and handed it to her.

"In general, or to him?" she inquired with hopeful display.

"I don't care. It's not like I have a chance in saving him so he can live normally anymore. His physical injuries are too grand for me to ever have him out as he used to be." The doctor said like it was a brief summary of the contents in the folder.

"Like, who gets bit by a shark and then floats ashore still alive? Or – or how about the fact his injury is dying but still flowing blood? What about the fact this man can go all day talking coherently but can't decide if his mother is alive or dead?"

"So, he is just gone then?" she asked concerned.

"Those are only his physical issues, love." He leans on the counter from which the folder came. "He has schizophrenic tendencies in his brain and early dementia as well. Those came after he started feeling the effects of our treatment." He continued almost admittingly. "I think."

"You think? What do you mean you think? How many tests have we ran?" she looked in the folder that was given to her by him. "Hundreds already! He has only been in our care for 6 months? How is that possible! He was found in December of 1999.

Without knowing when he started his journey alone at sea, he has been feeling these injuries for half a year, and we cannot figure out how it isn't healing *or* what is wrong with his mind?"

"Pretty much. Well said, Nurse Härkören." He said coldly to her. Not a care in the slightest.

"What's that compared to..." she started speaking before being interrupted by an alert buzzing overhead. The loud, interrupting alert beckoned for them like a soldier to peace. They went together to tend to the revealing problem. Upon reaching the room that started the buzz, they found Miska standing up and peering out of the window. He stood motionless, almost dead still. Not a muscle on his stitched, bruised wounds twitched.

"Strange that his wounds haven't healed by now." The doctor muttered under his breath.

"Not the problem here, doctor." she eagerly intruded on the doctor's first observation.

She had thought and pondered for a moment on how to approach without scaring Miska. The room filled with silence and awkwardness. The tension and awkwardness were taunting her to move while the doctor stood behind her staring rudely.

"Miska? What are you doing?" She finally asked.

The room grew even quieter as it ate her words. After what felt like forever, reality maybe a minute or two, a voice chimed up.

"There is a man down there staring back. He is scaring me." Miska croaked out while staying perfectly still in the window.

"May I approach you, Miska?" The doctor sought an answer. Hopeful for compliance, the doctor took a step quietly until Miska agreed to the request. The doctor copied him in glaring out of the window.

"Miska, there isn't anyone there." He said with concern in his voice.

"Yes, there is. Right there. In plain sight he stands." Miska said in an assuring manner. The dead of the night was unstirred of life. The streetlights illuminated under Miska. This room sat on the second floor with a view of the street in front of the hospital. Nobody lurked in the darkness at this hour, not a soul. No wolves howling, shadows creeping, or people pacing.

"Tell me about this man, Miska." She asked from the doorway to the room while the doctor looked for this mysterious figure.

"He is tall, wielding a knife, a shark tooth necklace. He has dark hair, it's long. A grey beard with beady eyes. He has a large part of his side missing. He matches me! That's so lovely, but it looks painful. He isn't covering it. It's leaking all over the side of the road. That's so inconsiderate. Wonder if he'll say sorry. Is he spying on me?"

"Why would that man say sorry, Miska?" The doctor asked while drastically more confused than before. 'What would that man have to be sorry for' he thought to himself, for he has not done anything other than stand there according to Miska.

"He bled on the road. Other people must see that and all. Not that it is rude, but it is now no longer a private problem or under your care, Doctor." Miska answered with an innocent gander in his voice. 'Apologize for bleeding'? How preposterous the doctor thought along with the nurse.

Why should anyone be ashamed of a problem such as that? Would he apologize for someone cutting his throat and taking his final breath as he bled on their shirt? Why should he? The thought process of Miska surely is perplexing and a rollercoaster worth of thoughts and ideas. It demonstrated itself uniquely to others, even if it was as concerningly tarnished with issues and narcotics.

"Anything else you, see?" The doctor asked while giving a glance back to the nurse and ignoring the final question that was returned to him. A glance that she still hates. A glance of mockery but power; it demonstrated his point entirely on the dire situation this man was in.

"He looks like me." Miska said coldly. A gust of abrupt cold air shot through the room when Miska spoke. The silence creeped in even more. The doctor stood cold and expressionless. I stood cold and expressionless. How does one respond to this? She cared about this man so much by now, but he has so many issues that are just unable to be solved. She is haunted by how his voice edged off and seized that moment of clarity. That room still feels that same way. It felt tranquilizing for the doctor and nurse.

-Unknown, 2000

VI

The Fish

We got to our fishing spot before noon together. It was beautiful. The sea rocked against the ship in a playful, tantalizing manner. A rhythm was made with the rocking, a peaceful rhythm. A rhythm of ease and softness. The scene stood majestically still to me. However, something was off. The clouds were stopped, and the sky felt plastered and untampered. It felt artificial and as though someone carefully picked it for just this moment.

"Are you okay, Miska? You've fallen silent again." Olari asked.

"Something just doesn't feel right today." I spoke. A game of back and forth of why and how erupted after I spoke. I thought of how the salt aroma felt slow and motionless. The clouds looked artificial and too perfectly still to me, but I couldn't say why. I couldn't articulate anything that I felt about it.

"It's a bright and sunny day! What could be wrong?" Jarmo said to me without a care in the entire deep blue. As brightly as he spoke with gestures and a smile, one could have assumed that everything was truly alright.

I had assured them both it was purely a feeling. For obvious reasons, I didn't - and don't - have the ability to fabricate anything into existence when I want. I casted my rod to the water, but I noticed something strange, very strange. The water wasn't crashing or moving. The thrill and beauty of the ocean's waves were gone.

We were sailors with no sea to move on. How was I the only sane person on this vessel to notice the drastic, disastrous change? I knew the feeling was growing before I even noticed the water was like a still-life painting. The clouds and sun were stuck too. I knew this wasn't as surreal as it was meant to be. I look at Olari and Jarmo. Based on their small talk and joy to be fishing together, I had concluded that they've really, truly not noticed.

"Why isn't the water moving?" I had asked with a tone of anger and annoyance to the two while growing confused. They had looked at each other before gazing at me. They stammered and can't decide together which is going to respond and answer first.

"Out with it, I cannot hear two conversations at the same time. Don't talk over each other now. How about you, Jarmo, you go first." I said as I took control of the confessions. I felt like an investigator picking with person was to have the hammer of questions struck to their mind first.

"Look, Miska." Jarmo finally decided to take charge and respond to me with a fatherly tone. "This is not real."

"What do you mean? I'm here obviously. I've smelt the salt and felt the heat. I heard the waves and even the weight of the fishing rod is in my hands." I said with a great deal of confusion in my voice, but still leading on that I knew something was not quite right. A pleasant mixture of certain but uncertain, the sun with the move, the cold with heat. The knowledge but unknown.

"No, you don't. It's all a dream that you've had before. We've never been here with you truly. This delicate dance of reality to illusion, you sleep. I – and Olari – speak and guide from the shadows of your mind. I'd implore you to wake up, but you cannot. You're sick by the hands of God you are." He continued with more. He gestured to compliment how he spoke. I was beyond caught off guard. What does any of that even mean?

How do you process and work that through your mind at all? Speechless was I, but I made sense somewhat quickly and stood silent.

"We've said too much, but we cannot stand what happens next with you. So, we will disappear from this dream. Keep fishing, younger me." Jarmo said to me. I tried to stop him from continuing on to ask what he meant by 'younger me'.

"Goodbye, older me." Olari waved to me before letting me intrude. They both faded away quickly to the air without answering what they meant. I struggled to speak to any organic being - which included myself.

I had a difficult time catching my breath and watching the motionless waves. By the hands of God? What have I done? My rod pulled on my hands abruptly, and I quickly reacted to pull in whatever fought on the line. I no longer checked the sky and waves to see the clarity in movement. I fought and fought and fought just to finally see the fish I won. It was that glowing fish again. The one that spoke in rhyme.

My stomach rumbled with excitement, courage, and the marvelous victory over the fish. I didn't and don't hate my life you impoverished, unimportant fish! I remembered quickly I had a portable grill for this exact instance. I grasped my knife with a smile and began skinning my free meal. I fired up and let the grill warm right on up. I began cooking the skinned fillet with its bone and all.

No longer you glowed, you idiotic symbol. I hate you! I hated, hate, will hate, forever hate you! You speak of nothing relating to me. How dare you assume my choices were not made with my interests along as others! For one to assume that is selfish. My habits are made, tailored, and worked for with my desires and others taken into account. I want happiness! I deserve it! Not your daft babbling telling me what I should believe!

As I was out to sea, I had no seasoning or precautions. I was on my own. Time passed and I was fishing no more but sailing alone. My mood had changed drastically after I thought more on what Jarmo and Olari admitted to me. What were they talking about? I am real, right? I started to feel sick.

I glanced down to the half-eaten fish. Its glow still gone. My vision blurred in and out when looking. A premonition flashed in my head. I saw my vessel in pieces without me on it.

I remembered just then, but why couldn't I before? I had to sail quicker! I needed to get back to land! My heart pounded with uncontrollable passion that said, "Faster, Miska, he's coming!"

The food I ate earlier, that fish, made my stomach churn and tie itself to knots. The water got faster, and waves rushed higher. They were no longer playing with my ship. A strong gust of wind grabbed the edge of my ship. It turned and nearly threw me overboard for the mysteries beneath to claw and grab at me. My sail's seams yelped and whistled as they tore from a damning wind. My head spun and lurked deeply in itself.

As if it hoped to die faster than me behind my own eyes. I saw the shoreline, but I was unsure where I was or what I believed to be real. Once more, the wind slapped against my slim-bodied vessel and grabbed at the edge. It pushed and pulled until it soaked me in salt.

I saw the top of my ship upside down. I was falling. So much so, I almost fell in love with sinking. I did get comfortable and felt at ease. The water was warm to me. It was comforting. The deep blue's hug froze my ambition with a familiar feeling. I've fallen before, but at that moment it felt right.

An enormous beast emerged and roared so loud it surrounded and vibrated my mere being as I fell. The salt hurt my eyes when I aimed my gaze to the source of all hate. I felt a brackish push and angry huffs coming to my side. A sharp pain shot through my hips and straight to my brain.

I tried to yell and scream with all my might and motivation left in my heart, but no matter which muscle I stole my energy from, I couldn't manage a sound. My brain was flooding and glooming with darkness. I've lost my thoughts at that moment. I rammed my hands at the source of the furious jaws of spite. I panicked and tried again at screaming to hopefully scare the beast off of me, but it kept going until its own satisfaction was granted. God's grace was the only savior of me now.

-Miska Korpi, 19...

꩜

He is doing it again. He is writing again. He is scribbling with graphite yet again. I am watching him write down whatever he believes at this point. After last night, I cannot decide if this is what I want to do. I am watching a person die slowly, but he doesn't know it.

They say people get a burst of energy before they die. Was that energy to stand in the windowsill yesterday that burst? Is Miska Korpi about to leave and meet the peace he should have? I don't know. As a medical worker, I cannot answer this question. I no longer know anymore.

He has survived being sank, a shark bite, his literal flesh dying on his bones, his prison he calls this comfortable bed and medicine, and hallucinating. What is next anymore? What is real? Is Miska really real? I have a priest coming in to talk to him about what happened. Maybe he should start praying to God? Would a gift from God answer and solve this issue? Would his flesh resurrect on his bones? His sins and past be cleansed from his mind? He is asking for me to come talk to. He has never done that, but I will answer his request.

-Nurse Härkören, 2000

VII

What's that?

I started seeing things more often than before. Nobody even bothers to notice them either. Last night, I saw a face in the window. It was smiling at me. A warm smile of hope, a hopeful smile it was. A smile with a thousand, no, a million teeth. A smile in a smile. Yes, that is precisely what it was. It gave warmth, joy, happiness, darkness too.

It was a smile in a smile with a million teeth. I nearly forgot! Yesterday, I saw that same figure I saw before that was standing at the road in a vent with the knife. He gives me protection I think, but I still fear him. Why is he bothering me this way? He looks like he belongs with me, but I still don't want him near me or my bed.

This bed is my bed! How dare that he might even ponder about taking it. I hit someone over moving me off the bed to clean the sheets. They are my trophies for living here this long, and I deserve this bed. I deserve everything about this bed. The pillow, the sheets, the covers, the weird machinery tied to my arms. I belong to it as it belongs to me. The wall should be mine. How can I make the wall mine?

The wallpaper is hideous if that is wallpaper at all. The paint, yes, the paint is ugly. Can I repaint the wall of this room? I have money at home, but I don't think I can make it home and back before someone takes my bed. I'm not good at goodbyes either. That Nurse has helped me through so much.

I wonder if she would get me paint to repaint the ugly color wall. Maybe she could get this entire setup back to my house! I wonder where she has been. I haven't seen her, my nurse, in about 30 minutes.

How dare she? Has she replaced me? She has been so sweet, but she is still only my nurse. My nurse, my bed, my wall, my pillow, my blankets, and my sheets. Those are the only things I get in this place and that is that. How dare anybody think of even taking those from me! This is my room away from home. I will get it back to my house when I'm allowed. Yes, that wall will be coming too. I will defend the wall and room from outsiders who wish to take it from me.

- Miska, 2000

He hit me today. Not hard or in the face. It was out of fear I believe, but he has never shown any aggression toward me. I was alarmed and frightened too after that.

He hit my arm when I was reaching for the sheets to start taking them off to replace them. I am reaching the end. I need to clean him, or I get in trouble, and I tried to tell him that, but he didn't care. He says the bed is his bed now. He claims it is the only thing I don't take from him and he needs it. I don't know what to do, but I can't ask the doctor or other nurses because then it looks like I cannot make my own decisions.

This is so unfair! He scribbles all day in that stupid journal then freaks out at anything I do to try and help him recover or feel happy. Why is this my patient anyway? Why did I accept his transfer to my care and room? I should have said 'no, I have enough' because on top of Miska, I have like eleven others that need the same attention.

I wanted to get his mother here, but he is totally against that she is his mother. I caved and did ask for that priest, but in the middle of them talking, Miska started freaking out and yelling that he was trying to possess his soul with a cross. What malarky is that? Possessing him with a cross is beyond wild. The priest started praying to him after that, but Miska told him that the devil was welcome to his room but not getting that wretched bed. Frankly, I don't blame the priest for leaving after that. I need to get some rest for tomorrow; I just wanted to document my last thoughts on this page in my office before I went home.

-Nurse Härkören, 2000

VIII

Imprisoned

I awoke to an alarm brightly and obnoxious ringing. There were lights and countless people over me yelling to each other. They had weird fabric clothing. I was rolling through a building with voices everywhere voices could sit. My vision was pulsing in and out fighting the darkness.

I couldn't feel my limbs. My eyes and heart were shaking. My side hurt. The figures mumbled and yelled a bunch of random things over me while they moved me to a dimly lit room. I was not quite sure what happened after that turn in the hallway, but I woke up again hours later. I was tightly bandaged, and my arm had a couple things hooked up to it. I stared at the ceiling and sighed. I hadn't had much time to myself to collect my thoughts before an older women walked in with a nurse. I saw what they were now. I was – and am – in a hospital.

"Miska? What were you thinking! Being at sea alone?" She spat her anger at me so much so I could feel it physically.

"Who are you?" I inquired.

"Your mother! How dare you ask me that?" She said yo me as she sat down with great attitude.

"You are not my mother." I said confused. "She hasn't been around for a few years. She has short, dark hair and is taller."

"I was in my 50's then. I'm 62 now." She explained.

"Her name was Maija."

"That's why your name is Miska. It matched the M's."

"She had a husband! He was always with her." I said with a straight face.

"He died 6 years ago, Miska. You were at his funeral."

"I did no such thing. You are not her." I snapped with a bite to my words as I got more and more frustrated.

"I even brought ID and your documents to help the doctors." She said as she lost hope.

"You stole my documents? From my home? Thief!" I snapped more than before. I turned my head away from her.

The nurse chimed in and broke up our talk.

"Hey, now, Miss, mind if I talk with you outside the door?" The nurse asked. My so called 'mother' agreed and they left me alone. The tension in the air grew stiff and paused like the sea. Everything froze in an instant. I'll write more tomorrow. How dare that idiotic woman come in and tell me who my mother is. She isn't with us anymore. I am sure of it. She'd visit me if she was.

-Miska, 2000

I spoke with Miska's mother after he basically yelled at her for not looking like she did years ago. The doctors, and me in particular, observed this behavior with other dementia patients. After speaking with the rejected mother, there are zero documents about any memory issues regarding Mr. Korpi. The mother's conversation went as such.

"Why won't he talk to me regularly?" She asked me after closing the door.

"I..." I went with a pause to think more radically. "I'm unsure."

"Aren't you meant to figure it out? Why was he rushed here? Why can't he recall I've changed? His father dying even!" She went on with great levels of emotion. She started to cry a river like the deep sea called. She wept with her words. She gave her speech life.

"We just got him in here... He was bleeding out and missing a large part of his side. Confirmed shark attack. He shouldn't be alive, but here he is." I lied a bit to lighten the blow, but still tried to keep the facts in the statement.

"Please bring back the kid I knew him to be." She requested nicely while a tear formed on her face.

"We'll do everything we can. You've my word." I said with great uncertainty of whether he would be here tomorrow.

-Mikko, 2000, official report.

After watching this woman cry to me, some other medical workers, and random bystanders. I really shouldn't have gotten the priest. He couldn't handle his mother. What was I thinking? This looks so bad on me for bringing two visitors up just for him to freak out at both. But how do you help someone who can't recognize someone and outbursts like that? Is it necessary? It is really the best reaction he could enact right there? I don't know much about these mental issues but that surely cannot be an excuse for that behavior? Am I just ignorant or am I a jerk? What do I have left to do for him? I don't know, but since I cannot think of anything to write down, I am just going to set the pencil down and clean or whatever.

-Nurse Härkören, 2000

How dare she bring in that fiend that believes to be my family. My mother walked out on me after I started being happy. With my choices made, t's crossed and I's dotted, heart set out on the path meant for me, she left and insulted me as she did so.

I just made a choice with the money given to me after I earned it. I outlived the best person in my life, and I know for a fact that he would have chosen the same thing that my money went to. Though it was taken from me by her! I spent a not a fraction on my habits and metal tin before it was just gone. She reported me and that was it. I never saw her again. I know that woman is not her.

My mother is old, but not that old either. It's only been... how long has it been? I don't quite remember, but I know for a fact she was not her. The years wouldn't have been that kind to that wench of a mother I was associating with all those years ago.

She should be burnt at the stake, that witch, for what she had done to me after his passing. I loathe her with as much hate that fills a heart full. She is not going to be the one to speak with me again.

If it isn't my father, then I want neither. She changed after my dad's death. I am almost certain she murdered him and then played the victim card. She was always someone who would do something like that. God, she hated everything my dad did. I wonder why she even married him.

-Miska, 2000

IX

Gone

It's been six months of being stuck in this place. This place haunts me. In the dimly lit prison, shadows danced weirdly across the walls, casted by the flickering fluorescent lights overhead. The air hung heavy with the sterile glimmer and scent of antiseptic.

I'm constantly reminded of the adventure beyond this room. The bed, a solitary peninsula in a sea of linoleum, felt confining. From the bed, every sound echoed with surprising amounts of clarity from the soft shuffling of nurses in the corridor, the distant hum of medical equipment, an occasional muffled conversation the faded in an out like radio static.

For people confined here, anger rose beneath the surface, a bitter brew that boiled over at the slightest provocation. Days bled into each other marked only by the crappy routine. Meals delivered on the same hour by the minute. Medication brought to my bedside. Every single week bled into a twenty-four-hour cycle that grabbed me further within these walls, anger became a constant companion.

It becomes so strong that it was shield of hope to get through this. For now, there is only pain, anger, and a constant reminder of captivity. I had the world's seas under my feet. What happened? How does a sailor end up in the hospital like this. What did I do? Trip and fall off the ship and nearly drown? It's hard to remember what happened. It is like I was never there when it did happen. I'm upset and hurt, bruised and battered, crying but dry, stiff but still. I am utterly confined like a pirate too frightened to steal. I don't deserve this.

-Miska, 2000

It's late at night. Someone keeps knocking on my door and whispering, but I cannot make up what. A whisper that tickles my ears. They are whispering with a snicker between deep inhales. The faint speaking still ran from wall to wall in my room, but not more than a tip-toeing pace. Nobody is coming to ask them why, almost like they don't hear this going on. Maybe they are doing on purpose? Are they paying someone to stand at my door and whisper to keep me up at night? No! I won't let them win!

"Go away!" I yell loudly. I won't let that voice in and win. They want something. I don't know what they want, but I know it is something. What that thing is will not be known until too late, so therefore, I will protect everything in this room. All of these things are mine and will not be taken without my consent. The dim, speckled tiles on the ceiling start vibrating and shaking.

"Get out of the roof! I know you are there! This is all mine! Mine, I say, mine!" I made sure to note loud enough for the thing in the roof to hear. My cream-colored sheets grow soaked in my cold-clammy sweat. No, they are winning! How can I let this happen! Why am I so disappointing? My arms seize and simmer. My eyes dart left and right of the room. A tight sensation and pain erupted in my chest. They are in! They are in the room! They are winning! I cannot breathe. I'm writing as I panic in hopes that it'll calm me down enough to fight back against these things in the roof and at the door. I can never let these things win over me. I must keep fighting and protecting all that I have left. I am no longer going to let things take things from me. I may have lost to a shark, but I will not lose to anything else! I am no longer a sailor, but a pirate ready to hack and slash!

-Miska

The place is so easy-going at this time; not a sound or care in the world. He is writing more than usual. It is so quiet that I can hear the pencil scribbling. The clock ticking isn't even louder than that pencil. Speaking of which, it's two in the morning and he is still awake scribbling and screaming. Should I stop him and ask that he goes to sleep? I'm going to because I cannot let him awaken other patients that are on the same schedule he is.

I am not super concerned over the fact that he is yelling. I barely pay attention to it anymore. However, he didn't stop when I got into the room. He actually told me he was losing and they were winning. Who? I have no idea who they are, but I assured him that he shouldn't let them win. He should keep fighting but not to wake up others and have this battle quietly.

I tried to look for that journal, but right when he heard my footstep before I fully entered, he hid it somewhere and told me that he was not going to let me win.

Not too sure where he hid the journal, but it was gone by the time I rounded the corner. I don't think he has figured out there is a window in which I see what he is doing before being in the room. Hopefully he doesn't figure it out because then he might yell about that too. Something was different though, as I rounded the corner he was in a cold sweat. His sheets were soaked, and his heartrate was through the roof. I alerted the doctor who came and checked, but said he was fine. He was just spooked and that I should be more attentive and careful when approaching him. I think the doctor is blaming me for scaring Miska. As he usually does. I don't know what to do about that, but I am surely going to get that journal before the doctor does.

I've been taking care of this patient longer than the doctor has been looking at his documents regarding the tests done on him. I have some rounds and other people to look after, so I'll update this paper next time I come back.

-Nurse Härkören, 2000

X

Who is he?

For what it was worth, I saw him. I really did see him! That man in the vents, he peered. I know he did. I saw him through the vent cover, he sneered and snickered while crawling away. I tried not to mention him to anyone else, but I couldn't help myself.

I could not say nothing while I knew he was there. I told the nurse that tends ever so carefully to me. She grew very concerned when she looked up to the vent. I saw what I saw, and nobody could ever convince me otherwise.

I am not crazy, and I knew he was there. I still know that he is there. He laughs that nobody believes me because, frankly, he is right. Nobody does believe me. He visits me sometimes at night.

He tells me things that I wouldn't be told. Like, one time, he tried to tell me that the doctors think I have dementia and schizophrenia. That was funny. Me? Having mental problems? Never. It's impossible. I'm too healthy and too perfect to have mental issues. I was never, ever crazy.

I've made perfect decisions all my life! Another time, when the man in the vents visited me, he told me that I had little bugs crawling in my skin, but I am not crazy enough to believe *that*. I'm not stupidly crazy. Why would he even try to get me to believe that? What does that mean? Do I actually have little bugs that crawl in my skin? No, there is no way that that is even remotely true.

-Miska Korpi

I am losing patience and hope in this patient. I want to help him more and more every day, but he is going further and further in the deep end. How can I help someone who goes further down the well despite pulling the bucket up? It is like he doesn't want my help.

The doctor and I caught him up out of bed a few times. On the most recent occasion, he was staring at the window, not out of or standing at it, murmuring that something was a dumb idea of escape. Us – not knowing how to react or process – hearing this raised a lot of perplexion. He kept explaining – at that time – that the means of escape through the window via quantum tunneling is stupid and a waste of time. We let him continue talking and found that he was able to explain the concept very well. He explained to himself without our intervention that, "quantum tunneling was an idea in physics."

He further went on to state that, "quantum tunnelling, barrier penetration, or simply tunnelling is a quantum mechanical phenomenon in which an object such as an electron or atom passes through a potential energy barrier that, according to classical mechanics, should not be passable due to the object not having sufficient energy to pass or surmount the barrier."

He mentioned all of this without speaking to us and continuing to murmur to himself about the idea being stupid. Upon asking and getting his attention, however, he was unable to justify or even mention the idea he was just speaking of.

He told the doctor and I that he was no scientist and thought we were trying to get him to join a cult we had made in the hospital of dumb ideas.

Another time that we caught him out of bed, we walked up on him during the night hours of rounds and he was spaced out.

I asked him, "Are you alright, Miska?" I was very concerned, and it showed through in my voice.

He met my question with, "Who is Miska?" He had a stone cold, hollow voice that had no soul. There was no heart below his vocal cords, no glimmer in his eye of life, no expression of distress, no hopeful smile like he had the day he arrived, his skin was losing life and discolored, he was holding his side like the pain returned. I was distraught. The man in front of me was not the man I met.

I wanted to hug him and say, 'it will all be alright', but I couldn't ensure that. He had no dream in his mind, no heart in his chest, no stability in his life, no shine in his eyes, no stargazer look, no color in him, no desire for the future.

"Although I am not Miska, that name brings me sorrow and woe. Deep, deep woe, and I request that it not be said to me again." He told me and the doctor as he stood more vertical and let his hand fall off his side, limp.

"Alright, Sir, then I must bring you back to your room and have you lay back down."

"I don't live here though. Why would I lay down?" He responded concerned and with little desire and wish to follow me. His voice stung knowing it was the man I met and helped all this time just disappearing in front of me. He was nothing like the man I helped those months ago. The man I knew was lively and determined to get through this to meet the awaiting sea with open arms. This man has an aura of woe lingering over him at all times that radiates to all the passersby. An aura that brought the bad times in your life forward for all to see again. This aura weighed at least a ton and weighed in itself on your chest. It grasped at your breath to choke the sorrow to right behind your eyes. You know? It was a toxic grasp. Whether the familiarity of the grasp depended on who felt this weight within this aura. The air was eradicated in the vicinity of it. It was gloomy when you stood next to this new version of him.

-Nurse Härkören, 2000

XI

I died

There lay Miska Korpi after his last night in that hospital. I – an all-powerful being – meant not to harm but to punish. I got carried away with my punishment. He suffered in a way I'd not wish upon the evilest criminal.

I'm sorry, God. I failed you. I controlled more than you allotted me and killed a man. I hope you can forgive me, Father Ukko. After abandoning his home, friends, and mother for his addiction to booze. He sailed alone and poached all kinds of fish.

One faithful day, I tried to warn him to stop by giving a godly grace of light to a fish. Oh, the fish I bestowed upon him. A glowing fish with wisdom words asking the questions philosophers ask themselves. We all wonder these questions.

Active mystery. However, after all the problems I gave this man, on purpose and accident, he retaliated and lived on. Medical practitioners fought to cure the curse I set on this problematic individual. I wish I can live and continue my duties and seek forgiveness for making a mistake to man that hurt someone. I am sorry, Ukko, Miska, and Miska's mother.

I sign as the person I destroyed.

-Miska

He had another burst of energy today. Miska stood up, went to the windowsill, crouched, and starting writing in his journal that he has had for the last however knows how long. I watched him write in that journal slowly and ominously for about 2 hours. I had to pause my writing as he fell on his side and wasn't moving.

He lost his pulse, and his eyes were no longer straining to look up at me. He was limp and gone. I called the doctor immediately while asking for help to resuscitate him on his bed. He wasn't heavy, as he was refusing most meals, I had brought him saying he wasn't allowed to eat anymore.

I no longer will be writing in secret because I actually feel this writing was out of spite for Miska writing without anyone else knowing. I think the blame is all mine for him passing and suffering. If he had suffered from anything other than his conditions, it was my fault. I was spiteful and ignorant.

-Nurse Härkören, 2000

⮌

10:45 am;

This is the doctor that worked with Mr. Korpi. I'm making this statement to inform your mind and heart of the dire mishappenings your son met.

I regret to say your son has passed. I'm so distraught that I am unable to face you in person to say. Also, scheduling to meet you was – and still is – much more difficult. His case was much more complicated than we prepared. Early on, he faced mental challenges. We found a journal he wrote in regularly suggesting he was seeing things. Based on his writings, it is evident to deduce Miska Korpi suffered memory and mental difficulties. A test was taken right before he passed, showing signs of Schizophrenia and early stages of Dementia. However, neither of these issues were traditional. He wasn't experiencing every symptom of either condition, but when he had an episode, he could describe each detail in a great level of detail. His expression of fear, confusion, and even sadness and bluntness were surreal. A very, very unfortunate case that will forever hold questions inside this hospital. I send my regards, Miss.

-Doctor

www.ingramcontent.com/pod-product-compliance
Lightning Source LLC
Chambersburg PA
CBHW022054170626
46808CB00003B/1468